God Calls Our Name

God Calls Our Name

Cover design by Kent Grey-Hesselbein,
KGB Design Studio
Manchester, TN, USA
http://kghdesign.nvaazion.com/

God Calls

Our Name

Terri Thomas St. Clair

Edited by

Stan St. Clair

God Calls Our Name

ISBN 978-0-9826302-5-9

Printed in the United States of America
St. Clair Publications
P. O. Box 726
Mc Minnville, TN 37111-0726, USA

http://stan.stclair.net

CONTENTS

Dedication

I would like to dedicate this final book of the trilogy to my husband, Roger, who loves me unconditionally, lets me know how much he adores me, and makes me feel beautiful, even on my un-lovely days. He is a wonderful father to our daughter, Melissa, and our son, Eric. He is a great Pawpaw to our precious grandchildren, Jonathan and Abby, and a good father-in-law to Jon, Sr. He has walked before us as a faithful servant of the Lord.

I love you, Rog.

Chapter One

It's been a month since the episode on the mountain. Hannah and Melissa are doing well. The Social Services Department placed both in foster care until their mom is well enough to take care of them. Daniel and I were pleased that they both are in the same home. The last we heard, they were adjusting and seemed to be happy. Hannah has been in therapy and still hasn't mentioned her baby. Roger said he felt it was just a matter of time and she would talk about it.

Ida and Jake came back to the trailer when Roger and Chris took turns going up there. Chris had him come in for further testing and found out that he did indeed have cancer. Ida came with him to the hospital for the surgery. Chris said he did remarkably well with the surgery, and was tolerating the chemotherapy and radiation pretty good, and seems to think he got all the cancer and his prognosis for complete healing is a wait-and-see game. The hospital was very kind to Ida and allowed her to stay right in the room with him.

Daniel and I have decided to take the RV back up to the mountains. My nausea has abated and I've been feeling wonderful, so Daniel agreed to let me go. He said we would re-evaluate the "little campers" when it's time to go. I know he watches me closely because he loves me and his babies. They have been moving like crazy. Daniel checks out the heartbeats almost every night. I love to watch his face light up when he locates them and speaks sweet words of encouragement to his "little campers," as he so lovingly calls them. I feel rested since the episode in the mountains.

I love our mountaintop home and have really enjoyed working in the flower garden. Mandy spoils me rotten and is always asking me questions about how I'm feeling and what is happening with the little ones. I told her we can hear their hearts beat and that I'm feeling them move. My tummy is expanding to the point you can definitely tell I'm pregnant. Mom Scott took me shopping for maternity clothes the other day, and can't wait for me to start decorating the nursery. I promised her we wouldn't leave her out of anything.

I love the new family God gave me and treasure the times we have together. Grandma Scott is doing well and keeps the community informed about how I'm doing.

I was heading out into the yard to work in the flowerbed when I heard the phone ring. It had to be Daniel, I thought. He phones many times a day just to tell me he loves me and ask about his campers.

"Hi sweetie, it's me. How would you like to take a little trip with me to Stony Ridge to check out a patient? Someone called and said they are concerned about their mother. They live out of town and can't get to her. She hasn't answered her phone for a few days. So I told them I would go. They said they had heard about our medical trailer and hoped we could go. She is a diabetic and arthritic. Her son cares for her but no one has seen or heard from him either. Would you like to go?"

"Sure, do you want me to drive in and meet you?"

"No, I'll drive by and get you. It's right on the way. I'm not taking the big trailer this time."

"I'll be waiting for you. Bye, I love you."

"And I, you. See ya in a minute."

It took us about thirty minutes to reach the road she lived on. It was just about a mile off the main road. The driveway wound up behind the house. We parked and went around to the front. We knocked on all the doors, and tried to look in the windows and got no answer, so we went back to the front porch and knocked again. When we didn't get a response, we checked to see if the door was locked. Daniel turned the knob and the door opened easily.

"I hope this is the right house. I would hate to get shot for breaking and entering," he said with a half-hearted chuckle.

We called her name as we went so she wouldn't be frightened at our sudden appearance.

"Mrs. Akers, this is Doctor Scott," he called. "We're here to check on you."

"I'm in here." a voice called weakly. We followed it into a living room at the back of her house. We found a frail little woman sitting in a recliner.

"Pardon me fer not gettin' up. This old arthritis got me down. It's just about taken over my whole body."

"We thought we would drop by and see how you're doing."

"Did my son send ya?" she asked with concern in her voice.

"No, actually it was your daughter. She said she couldn't hear from you and was worried."

"Have ya'll seen my son? I thought he was goin' to the doctor, but he never did come back. I've been stuck in this here cher fer two days." She began to cry then.

"We haven't seen your son. You haven't had any food or water?" She shook her head and continued to cry softly.

"Well, actually the little neighbor boy came by and brung me some food that his mama sent. And I went to the bathroom with a walker. I had my phone turned off 'cause I couldn't pay the bill, so that's why my daughter couldn't reach me."

"Why didn't you tell him to call for help?" Daniel gently questioned her.

"I thought my boy was a-comin' any minute, but he never did."

"When was the last time you ate, Mrs. Akers?" Daniel asked.

"Last night I ran out of food, what th' boy brung. My son usually takes me out to get food, but he ain't come home."

"You're diabetic, isn't that correct?"

"Yeah, I take pills, I don't do shots."

"I bet you're not feeling too good right now, are you?"

"No, I ain't," she said, starting to cry again.

"Libby, take the van down to that little store we saw right up the road and get Mrs. Akers a snack and something to drink. While you're there use their telephone and call an ambulance. I'm pretty sure she's dehydrated. We need to get some fluids started. I'll follow you out and get the monitor for her blood sugar levels."

Daniel followed me out to the van after assuring Mrs. Akers that he would come right back.

"Honey, that car in the driveway; I wonder if it could be the son's car?" Daniel said.

"I don't know, but we should find out."

"Why don't you call the police while you're there? It's been a long time for him to leave an invalid mom. Explain the situation to them and see if they might do some checking."

"Okay, I'll be back as soon as I can."

"Be careful honey," he called after me.

It didn't take me long to get to the store and call the officials. They said help was on its way. The paramedics said they would notify the police.

I hurried into the house with the purchase. Daniel had finished his exam by the time I returned. He had given her a shot of insulin and had gotten her some water.

"Here's some food, honey. They sold hot-dogs, so I got one of those and a coke, some chips and a Moon Pie."

"She's about ready for some."

"That's what I got for me. Did you want me to bring her food?" I asked jokingly. "I wasn't sure about the Moon Pie, but I thought she might need something with sugar in it.

"A Moon Pie? Why would you think this poor hungry lady would want a Moon Pie?

"Could this be because you've been craving Moon Pies?" he asked, grinning at me. "Hmm, is that why there are two Moon Pies in this bag?" he said, taking the food out.

"I thought the little campers might be hungry," I said, smiling impishly at him.

He opened the food while I got a plate from the kitchen.

She seemed to like the attention she was being given.

We heard the siren of the ambulance coming up the lane to her house.

"I'll go out to meet them." Daniel said, rising to his feet.

He was gone just a few minutes and came in with the policeman beside him.

"Mrs. Akers, this policeman is going to try to help us find your son. So if you could answer a few questions it would help."

"Okay, I'll try."

"Mrs. Akers, I'm Sheriff Lyons, I won't be very long. When was the last time you saw your son?"

"It was two days ago. He weren't feelin' too good and was a-goin' to go to the hospital and see what was wrong. I was thinkin' he might be in the hospital. You see, my phone's been cut off and he wouldn't have no way to call me."

"What color car does he have?" the policeman inquired.

"It's a dark red. I'm not sure what ya call it, but it just had two doors."

"Is it possible that he could have gone to the hospital with someone else?"

"No, he wouldn't a-done that without tellin' me."

"So, when he left you he told you he was sick?"

"Yes. He said he thought it just might be indigestion."

"Well, we're going to go outside and see if we can call the hospital to see if he went there. What is his name?"

"His name is David Lee Akers."

"Thank you, Mrs. Akers," the policeman said, stepping away from her and out to the porch.

Daniel and I followed him out. He told us that the car in the driveway was her son's. If the hospital check was negative they were going to take a look around the property to see if they could turn up any clues.

While the paramedics continued getting her ready for transport, we stood on the porch and listened to the policeman call his office to get them to do the hospital check.

"They are going to radio me back when they find out," he told us.

About ten minutes had elapsed when the radio squawked. When he finished, he returned to the porch where we were standing.

"He ain't in any of the ones they checked. Me and my deputy 're gonna look around. Do you think she's stable enough for ya'll to wait? I might need to ask her a question or two."

"Yeah, she's stable, just needs some fluids. She'll be okay."

Daniel and I went in to convey the message to the attendants.

"I'd like for you to start and IV on her," he told the ambulance attendant. "She may be a little dehydrated, so pushing some fluids isn't going to hurt. The policeman wants us to wait just a bit in case they need to ask her some more questions."

"Dr. Scott, I'm not sure about leavin', 'cause David Lee might come home and be worried 'bout me."

"We can leave a note on the door telling him where to find you."

"Okay, if ya think it's alright," she said, still not quite sure she should.

The policeman came to the door and motioned Daniel outside. I followed to see what was going on.

"Well, we found him out back and he is dead. They have an outside toilet and I guess he was going to go there before he left to see the doctor. We found him lying half in, half outside the toilet. I would think maybe it was a heart attack, or something like that. It seemed he went fast. I'll call the coroner to come pick him up," he said.

"Man," Daniel said, "I sure wasn't expecting that. I hate to have to deliver this message."

"I can if you want me to," the policeman said.

"No, I can do it. I just hate to," he answered.

"The coroner's on his way, he said, tipping his hat before walking away."

"Mrs. Akers, they found your son."

"Oh, good, I'm gonna have to scold him fer not coming back. Wher' is he?" The worry seemed to lift from her face.

Daniel and I walked up on either side of the stretcher and each held a hand.

"He won't be coming in to see you. They found him dead out back. He must have had a heart attack. We should know for sure after an autopsy. He probably died instantly."

"No...." she wailed, as her hands flew up to cover her face. "No, please tell me yer kiddin'."

"I wouldn't kid you about something so serious," Daniel said tenderly.

"He was my only son. I have a daughter not too far away." She continued to sob.

Daniel gave her a sedative to calm her for the ride to the hospital.

"Mrs. Akers, you're going to be fine. I'll call your daughter when we get to the hospital and she will come and be with you."

"Okay," she mumbled on her way out.

Daniel gathered his things and we went to the van.

"I have to go to the office and write a report. Would you like to go with me?"

"Sure," I said, smiling at him.

"Are you tired?" he asked, patting my knee.

"No, I feel great. Well, actually I do feel a little tired. I wanted Mrs. Akers Moon Pie really bad," I told him, smiling up at him as we walked to the car.

"I thought you got one," he said, looking at me.

"I did eat that one. Don't forget there are two little campers. They don't like to share," I said, laughing.

"I'll get you another one at the next store we come to, and let me guess, you would like to have a Pepsi too, right?"

"You read me like a book."

True to his word, he stopped and got me not one, but two more—and a Pepsi.

"This is a spare for later, so I don't have to get up at midnight and try to find you one. Of all the things you could crave, I can't believe it's Moon Pies."

"And Pepsi," I added.

"What happened to pickles and ice cream?"

"That's disgusting, who would like pickles and ice cream?"

"The same pregnant women that would crave Moon Pies."

I had the wrapper off and was eating it before we were even on the road.

"Is it good?" Daniel said, turning to look at me.

"UMMMM, the best I've ever had."

"You said that when you ate the last one," he said, grinning at me.

"I know, but they just seem to get better."

"I'm going to have to make sure you eat your vegetables," he said sternly.

"Oh, Daddy, do I have to?" I said, pouting.

"Mandy takes notes. She will tell me if you don't."

"You two conspire against me," I said, kissing his hand.

"Did you get Moon Pie on me?" he said, inspecting the back of his hand.

"No, that's from my sweet lips," I said, smiling at him.

Chapter Two

Before we knew it, we were at the clinic. Daniel went into his office and I laid on the love seat in the waiting room. Daniel turned the music on so I could hear it on the speakers. It wasn't long before I was sound asleep.

It seemed I had just fallen asleep when Daniel was gently calling my name.

"Time to wake up, little Moon Pie, time to go home," he said, gently kissing me. "Just checking for Moon Pie."

He helped me to my feet and guided me to the car.

"I guess I was more tired than I thought."

"I talked with Mrs. Akers' daughter and she is going right to the hospital. I talked with the hospital and they had her settled in."

"I bailed out on you."

"Yeah, you had your Moon Pie fix and went right to sleep. Now when the babies come and Mommy tells them they can't have a lot of sugar, I'm going to tell them all about your little cravings."

"You must be starving," I said with concern.

"No, I ate your other Moon Pie," he said sheepishly.

"You ate *my* Moon Pie? Now, what am I going to do for one later?"

"You'll just have to do without, because Daddy's not going on a Moon Pie run tonight."

"The babies are moving like crazy," I said, putting my hand over my stomach.

"They probably are having a sugar rush."

When we got home, Mandy had our dinner warming in the oven for us.

After a quick dinner we thanked Mandy for taking such good care of us, and headed up the stairs arm-in-arm to our bedroom. We hadn't been asleep long before the phone rang. Daniel muttered to himself as he answered it. I never answer at night because they are usually for Daniel.

"Hello, oh, Hazel, yes, of course I remember you. How are you?" He asked, still groggy from sleep.

"When did this happen? Of course we will, but it won't be until morning. Tell her we will be there as soon as possible. Good bye."

"What happened?" I asked, dreading the answer.

"I'm afraid it's your grandmother. Hazel says she is real sick and refuses to go to the doctor. She wants us to come and check in on her. She said she's been in bed for several days and refuses to get up. Hazel said she's been asking for us."

"Can you get free to go with me?"

"Do you think I would let you go alone? I'm sure the group can handle things for me."

"Honey, I need to talk to her about her soul. Pray that God will tender her heart."

Neither one of us seemed to sleep well, so we were up early, and were on the road at daybreak. I didn't pack much for us. I figured we wouldn't be long.

By late morning we were pulling into her overgrown driveway. We made our way over the footbridge without one dog barking. *That was unusual,* I thought to myself.

"I wonder where the dogs are. I hope they aren't sneaking up on us," Daniel said, looking over his shoulder.

"They're probably tied. We'll assume so anyway."

Hazel met us at the door with a relieved expression on her face.

"I'm so glad y'all're finally here. She ain't doin' so good. I've even had the medicine lady across the holler make her up some herbs and teas, but, ain't none hepped much. I think she needs a real doctor. She just keeps a-sayin' Daniel will come take kere of me. She's been talkin' about Rose and

'Lisbeth a lot. I'm glad ya got here 'afore she passed. It would a-been a shame fer her to pass without seein' 'Lisbeth one more time."

We followed her down the hall to the bedroom. The room was dark except for one dim light bulb on the shade-less lamp by her bed. The room was hot and had a horrible stench. I felt waves of nausea and willed it to stay down.

She looked as if she had lost a lot of weight since the last time we saw her.

"Rachel, are ya awake? Daniel and 'Lisbeth are here to see ya," Hazel said.

Daniel moved up beside her and felt her pulse. He had brought his medical bag in and had it opened. He took the stethoscope out to check her heart and lungs.

"Don't go foolin' with me boy, I ain't got long fer this here world. I want to go see Rose Ann. Hits been sech a long, long spell since I seed her. My heart don't want to go on no more."

Daniel kept checking her while she talked.

"Can you take a deep breath for me?"

"Ain't got no breath."

"Try to," he encouraged.

She drew a shallow breath and coughed a rasping cough. I had heard this sound so many times in my nursing career. The mountain people called it the "death rattle."

He took her blood pressure and looked at me. The look I saw on his face told me what I suspected was true.

"'Lisbeth, I was a-hopin' you would make it 'afor I was gone. It's been a hard, hard life," she said with tears trickling down the tributaries of wrinkles on her weathered face.

"Grandmother Rachel, I've got something I need to tell you.

"What is it, chile?" she said, barely above a whisper.

"There is someone who loves you so much."

"No one I know of loves me, 'cept you maybe."

"He has loved you all your life, his name is Jesus."

"I know all about Jesus, but he jest loves good people. I've been too mean fer him to love me." She began to cry harder and her frail body trembled beneath the thin covers over her.

"That's the beautiful part," I said, wiping away her tears. "He came to give a new life to those that call on his name."

"My life is almost over, he cain't give me a new one. I'm too old."

"This new life is forever, Grandma, Jesus died on the cross so we could live forever in heaven. All you have to do is ask him to come into your heart and save you."

"I'm too bad, chile. I ain't been very good, it's too late fer me, but I thank ya fer tellin' me."

"It's never too late to call on the name of Jesus. Just pray and ask him to come in and he will.

Will you pray, Grandma, will you pray?" I said, with tears running down my face.

"Don't cry, chile," she said, reaching up with her trembling hand to wipe my tears. "Do you really think Jesus might fergive me fer all the bad things I done?"

"I know he will. He promised that those that call on his name, he will save."

"How?" she said, barely above a whisper.

I proceeded to tell her how to pray, and to my wonderment I heard her whisper the words asking Jesus to come in and save her.

"Did you really mean that prayer, Grandma?" I asked though my tears.

"As best as I know how, I meant ever' word. "Will I be able to go wher' Rose went?"

"Yes, you will live forever with her, and one day I will join you and Rose, and we will have a long time to get to know each other. But right now, you need to rest."

"I ain't got time. There's sumpthin' I gotta say 'fore I rest. In the top drawer of that chester drawer is a little notebook yer mama kept while she was a-carryin' ya. She wrote things in it that ya might want to read. That's all I got to give ya of her'n. I'm sorry I let my pride and hate git in the way of lovin' ya. I wish I had more time to know ya. Maybe in heaven we will," she said with a slight smile on her face. Her voice was getting weaker with every word she spoke.

"I'll be goin' soon."

"Don't say that, you might have a long time," I told her.

I went to the dresser and tried to open the top drawer. The wood was damp and difficult to pull open. Daniel came over and gave it a big tug and it slowly gave way. I rummaged around in the junk-filled drawer until I found a little brown bag with a rubber band wrapped around it. It was the only thing in the drawer that looked like it could be what I was looking for. I held it up where my grand-mother could see it.

"Is this it?" I said, holding it up.

She strained to lift her head off the pillow.

"Yes, that's it. I put it in the bag to hold it together. It's as old as you are. It's all I had to hold onto."

I could almost see the hardness leave her face and a softness take its place after she prayed for Jesus to save her. She had had a rough life, and now she would move on to heaven, to share an eternity filled with love and happiness. Too bad she didn't have any of that here on earth. Her life had been filled with hatred and bitterness. She was unhappy and tried to make everyone else as sad as she was. Finally she would know what peace and happiness truly is.

I looked up and saw Daniel motion for me to come outside her room. As I was leaving, I saw where the awful stench was coming from. In the corner was a pot she had used for a toilet. I felt the wave of nausea return full force. I pushed Daniel out of the way and dashed for the front porch, barely making it in time.

"Hey sweetie, are you okay?" Daniel said as he reached me.

"I will be in just a minute. The smell really hit me hard. I don't think she has had a bath in a long time. I need to heat some water and give her one."

"Do you think you're up to it, honey?"

"Yeah, I just need a minute to get some fresh air."

"She doesn't have much time left, sweetheart. It sounds like congestive heart failure. She's full of fluid, and her blood pressure is sky high, I'm surprised she hasn't had a stroke yet."

"I guess we better get back inside," I said, turning to follow Daniel into the house.

"This child really needs you now, Lord, give me strength," I prayed.

I took some deep cleansing breaths before going back in. Daniel helped me get a pan of water ready and we carried it into the bedroom. We brought a kitchen chair to set the pan of water on.

"Grandmother, I'm going to give you a nice warm bath."

"No, I cain't let ya do that."

"I've never had the opportunity to do anything for you, so please let me do this."

I asked Hazel to bring me some clean clothes for her. I finally found a half-way clean towel and wash cloth. The only soap I could find was a bar of lye soap that the mountain people swore by. They washed both clothes and bodies with it. *I wish I had some good smelling soap to wash her in just so she could smell the sweetness*, I thought.

I took her clothes off one piece at a time and was careful to cover her so I wouldn't embarrass her, washing one area and covering her before starting another area. I took my time and lovingly and tenderly bathed her. I talked to her as I bathed her to take her mind off washing her more embarrassing parts.

Tears began to flow freely from her eyes. She covered her face with her hands to try to stop them.

"No one's ever been so nice to me," she cried.

Daniel hovered close by to help me turn her as I worked. I noticed once as I glanced over at him that his eyes were moist with tears as he watched the scene unfold before him.

"I wish I had had more time with you, but I didn't. One day, Grandmother Rachel, we'll have an eternity to get to know each other. How long have you been bedfast?"

"I took to my bed about a week ago. I had a bad spell with the flu. I ain't seemed to get over it."

"Did you see a doctor?"

"No, Hazel come over and put some kind of salve on me, and a onion poultice fer my chest. She gave me some herb medicine. That does about as good as goin' to the doctor. I used earth medicine all my life. I ain't got much longer." She wheezed with each breath. "Pray fer me, chile. Pray Jesus takes me soon. I hurt so bad."

Daniel stood silently beside me holding my hand, or gently rubbing my shoulder just enough to let me know he was there.

"I'll pray if you want me to," he said, looking tenderly into her eyes.

He knelt down by the side of her bed and took her hand, swollen with fluid that had gathered in her body with no place to go.

She labored so with each breath she took. It seemed each successive one was a little harder. She had so much fluid in her body that it was pushing out her skin in water blisters

"Thank ya fer comin', chile, and showin' me how to get to heaven. I wouldn't be goin' if it wasn't fer you," she said slowly, wheezing with each word. "I didn't mean to be a mean woman. It just seemed to happen. Ain't nobody keered fer me. Most people wished I'da died when my Rose died," she said weakly. "I didn't let nobody close to me, 'cause ifen ya do, ya open ya'self up to bein' hurt. Nobody ever loved me, nobody." She closed her eyes and tried to take some deep breaths; all she could manage was little short gasps. And tears were still flowing from her eyes.

I sat by her holding her hand.

"I love you, Grandmother Rachel, and Daniel loves you, and Jesus loves you. I'm sure Hazel loves you. She's stuck by you all these years."

"She's been a good friend, but I ain't."

"Why don't you just close your eyes and try to rest a little. When you're upset it makes it harder for you to breathe."

"Pray fer me, 'Lisbeth," she said without opening her eyes.

"Dear Heavenly Father, your child is ready to come home. You know how her life has been. She's ready to take her rest. The things you have waiting for her in your kingdom are beyond anything I could ever imagine. Thank you for allowing me to lead her to you. Ease her suffering and make her passing easy. Help her to feel your presence. Bring her joy and peace that she has never known before."

The room became totally quiet. In my mind I could feel the rush of angel wings as they came to carry her home. Her hand relaxed in mine. No labored breath now; she has taken her first breath of heavenly air. I wished for a moment that I had eyes to behold everything that just unfolded before me.

Daniel reached down and took my hand in his and helped me rise up to his outstretched arms.

"She's gone, sweetheart, she's finally at rest. I guess you prayed her into the presence of Jesus," he said, pulling me close to him.

"Take your rest, Grandmother Rachel. I'll see you when I get to heaven," I said as I wiped the tears from my eyes.

I was suddenly aware of Hazel sitting in a chair behind me. I had totally forgotten she was present. She was weeping softly into her handkerchief.

"She was as mean as a snake but I loved her. I guess I was the onliest one that took the time fer her. Under all that bitterness was a real needy soul afeered to love," she said, blowing her nose.

"Honey, we've got to go call the funeral home. There are things that have to be done, and I guess we're the only ones that can do them," Daniel said.

"Ya'll can use my phone," Hazel replied.

"Do you have a phone book where we could find the numbers to call?"

"Yeah, she wanted to be buried beside Rose. She's been a talkin' about what to do when the time come. She writ down some things the other day. She don't have no church or preacher, so I guess we can borry one from the fun'ral home."

I stayed there while Daniel went with Hazel to phone for the coroner to come pick up her body. At least she was clean. I sat by her bed and studied her face. It was lined with deep, furrowed wrinkles. Years of bitterness were etched there. Her once-black hair was streaked with a yellow-white color. She had it pulled back tightly into a little knot at her neck. It was slicked back with dirt and oil from days without a shampoo. *How sad,* I thought, *to be angry and bitter your whole life.*

I clutched the brown bag holding the notebook of my mother's journaling. I was glad she hadn't destroyed it. Maybe I could glean something about my mother. I heard Daniel coming back across the bridge. Strangely, I still didn't hear the dogs barking.

"Did you see the dogs outside?" I asked Daniel.

"Hazel said she gave them to a neighbor last week. She said she couldn't take care of them anymore. Hazel made the arrangements."

Daniel was able to stay and help me plan her funeral. We had opted for a graveside service. We picked out a pretty dress for her to wear. It wasn't fancy because she wasn't fancy. We tried to do what we thought she would like. Hazel gave us the paper she wrote her funeral arrangements on. It went something like this. "No singing just put me in the dirt. No fancy words fer I weren't fancy.'

I'm so thankful Mama told me about my grandmother. It was painful at first, but as I learned more and more, my soul was at ease. Getting to lead her to Jesus will be something that will stay with me eternally. *Mother, I did what you asked me to do, I found my grandmother and am sending her home for you to love and enjoy.*

The preacher from the funeral home came to the gravesite. Daniel and I placed a spray of roses and lilies of the valley over her coffin.

"Mrs. Scott, I believe you and Dr. Scott would like to say a few words," he said, looking at me.

"Yes, we would." I stood up and Daniel stood with me and held my hand.

"Grandmother Rachel, here we are, bidding you goodbye. I've just said hello and now I have to say goodbye. I'm sorry you lived a life full of pain and hatred. If only I could have brought the message of Jesus' love sooner. I hope you felt a little bit of love before you died. I'm sure that right now you're visiting with Rose. When I come home to heaven, we'll have an eternity to get to know each other. I carried the message my mother sent to you, the message of salvation. We were at the stroke of midnight, but you made it home. It scares me to think how close we came to losing you forever. You are learning all about Jesus now and how much he loves you. Thank you for the notebook. One day soon I'll read the message she left for me. I love you." I looked at Daniel and waited for him to speak.

"Grandmother Rachel, I became your grand-son when I married Elizabeth. I was the first to tell her of Rose. How painful it was for her to hear the story, but, how much more the pain must have been for you carrying the story in your heart for your whole life. How you must have longed for her. The guilt you must have had for giving her away. But now your burdens are lifted, and forevermore your burdens will be gone. I wish I could have made your last days a little less painful, but that wasn't meant to be. Take your rest now and we'll see you in heaven."

God Calls Our Name

It was a hot June day as we stood by her grave. The sun was beating down on us as we bid her goodbye. The blanket of roses and lilies that covered her casket held but a hint of the love I felt in my heart. It's a shame that these are probably the only flowers she has ever gotten. Maybe she can see them from heaven. Daniel started singing a song that I knew well and I joined him. I was so glad we could sing at her grave "It is Well with My Soul." Having witnessed her accepting the Savior, I could sing assuredly that everything was well with her soul. As we sang, a cool breeze came blowing by and left as quickly as it came. I think she was there to see that we were there for her.

"Hazel, would you like to say something?" the preacher kindly asked.

"No," she said, wiping her face with a large white handkerchief.

"Well, if we all agree, we will lay her to rest. May God give you peace."

God Calls Our Name

That was the end of the service. There were just the four of us at the gravesite. It was one of the saddest ones I've ever been to. I didn't have the overwhelming emotion I had when I lost David, or when I lost my mom and dad. The saddest part is that someone would come to the end of her life and only have three people, and the preacher, come to her funeral.

The only thing people will remember her for would be her bitterness, her anger, and the hardness of her spirit. What a legacy to leave behind. If she had only known sooner how much Jesus loved her and was willing to forgive her, how much happier she would have been. I wept for the lost years she had and for the grandmother I never knew.

"Goodbye, Grandmother Rachel," I said, laying a single rose on her coffin.

Daniel pulled me close to him and we walked arm-in-arm to our waiting car. The babies were kicking furiously as we stood by the grave. They never let me forget they were there.

God Calls Our Name

We saw Hazel to her house, and headed back toward our home. I laid the seat back to allow the babies more room to romp. It felt good to stretch out some. I cuddled up to the pillow I brought, hoping to rest some. The hum of the engine and the soft music on the radio put me right to sleep.

I dreamed I saw Rose with Rachel walking through a field of flowers holding hands. There were no words spoken, just the two of them strolling together.

I woke up about a half an hour from our house. I was surprised that I had slept so long, because I wasn't normally a car sleeper. I guess these two little ones made me more tired than I thought.

"Hey, sleepy head," Daniel said, smiling at me.

"Why didn't you wake me? I didn't mean to sleep so long."

"You just looked so cute lying there sleeping, I couldn't do it. I've listened to the radio, and thought about the little campers, so I haven't been lonely. How are you feeling?"

"Just tired, the babies have been rock and rolling today," I said with a chuckle.

Daniel placed his hand over my round tummy, and smiled at me.

"They've really been growing lately."

"Can you imagine what it's going to be like when the time comes for me to deliver?"

"You will be beautiful no matter what size you are." Daniel said, smiling at me.

One of them decided to kick right at the moment he had his hand there.

"Did you feel that?" he said in amazement.

"They've been at it all day. I think they wanted to show Daddy how strong they are."

"Football players, they will definitely be football players."

"Or ballerinas," I added. "I'm starving, I'm glad we're almost home. I'm going to go raid the refrigerator. Do you think Mandy got me some Moon Pies and Pepsi?"

"I hope so. I don't want to hear you whine when you want one and don't have it."

I hit him on the arm. "I don't whine, not much anyway."

"You don't whine. I was just teasing. Honey, I will buy you a store full of Moon Pies if that is what you and my babies want."

Chapter Three

It was late by the time we reached home. The first thing I did was go to the bathroom, and then found something to eat. Mandy knew we would be coming in and had fixed something she could warm easily for us. She always knew what we would need even before we asked. She was so precious to us and we really treasured her. She was so excited about the babies coming. Believe me; with two, she was going to be a godsend.

As soon as we finished, we headed upstairs to go to bed. I hoped I would be able to sleep after having slept so much on the way home. Daniel and I unloaded the suitcases. I took the brown paper bag that held the diary and laid it on the dresser. I wanted to have time to read it without interruptions. Daniel put the suitcases away and we climbed into bed.

The late supper must have supercharged the twins; they were kicking up a storm. Daniel turned over with his back to me and I scooted up real close to him and he could feel the twins kick him in the back.

"Okay, boys, quit kicking Daddy. It's time to go to sleep," he said with a chuckle.

It wasn't long before he was snoozing. I was still trying to get comfortable when the phone rang. He fumbled for it in the darkness, grumbling as he answered it.

"Dr. Scott here. Oh, hi Chris."

"We got in about 11:00."

It seemed whatever Chris was saying got Daniel's attention. He was silent for so long I thought he fell asleep, and then I heard him respond.

"Sure, if you need me I'll be right there."

"Oh, honey, do you have to go to the hospital?" I said, discouraged.

"Yeah, they're in emergency status. They've had a huge intake of patients and need all the doctors in. I hate not to go because they've covered for me a lot lately. He said he hated to call, but they are up to their eyeballs. Chris was headed for surgery when he called. With him in surgery it really will put the ER staff in a bind."

"What kind of emergency?"

"There was some kind of pile up on the interstate. I need to go hit the shower and try to wake up. Could you go fix me some coffee while I'm showering? It would help a great deal."

I fixed his coffee and put it in a thermos and headed back to bed. I lay there waiting for him to come kiss me goodbye. I hated it when he had to work late. The bed was so big and empty with him gone.

"I'll be back as soon as I can. Pray that this won't take long, and don't wait up," he said, then leaned and kissed my stomach. This had become a ritual as he would leave for work. He would always kiss my stomach, and tell the babies that he loved them.

After he left, I lay in the darkness for a long time trying to go to sleep and still couldn't. I went to the kitchen cupboard and got a Moon Pie and then a Pepsi from the fridge and headed back up to the bedroom. I figured if I was going to be awake, I would be happy. I took the brown paper bag holding the journal and settled down in the big recliner to read.

"We are going to learn about your grandmother," I said to the twins.

I sat my Moon Pie and Pepsi on the stand beside the chair. I carefully opened the bag and took the notebook out. Even though it was old, it was in remarkable condition.

I held it for a moment, contemplating what I would find. When she wrote this, she was carrying me and my sister. It's odd that I would be reading it as I carry my own twins. The notebook smelled musty from being kept in the drawer so long. I opened it and saw the ink was still fresh looking against the yellowing pages. It was written neatly and was precise. It seemed as if she took great care in recording the happenings of her pregnancy. It started out in August.

Chapter Four

August 1st. Diary, I'm so lonely not havin any friends, so mama got you fer me. I guess yer gonna be my friend. I ain't got much to rite today cepten it's awful hot. We got some new miners comin in the tavern at nite. Some are real cute, but she don't 'low me to talk to em. I still look when she ain't lookin. Well I'll rite more tomary.

Aug. 2nd. I turned 18 today. I wanted a cake but mama said she ain't got no time fer sech things. I jest want to feel special. I ain't never had no cake. I don't know, I thought it would be difernt this time. Theres this real cute man been makin eyes at me. I'm gonna talk to him tonite when mama gets busy.

August 3rd. I met that man. He was a dreamboat. Said I had the most beautifulist eyes he ever seed, and diary, he was sweet too. I realy liked talkin to him. Mama saw me and didn't say nuthin.

August 4th. Its hottern any day I ever seed. I'm really sad cause Randy went home today. Be back on

Sunday nite. I Cain't wait to see him agin. He shore does seem to like me.

I continued to read down through the month. From Rose's point of view, my daddy seemed to be really taken with this bronze-haired little Rose. So far they seemed to have spent many long hours talking. I gather from what I'm reading they are really enamored with each other. They seemed to have hit a low time in their lives at the same time. I could see the fall coming already. *Daddy, how could you have been so blind?* I thought.

August 20th I'm not sure zactly what's happennin to me and Randy. He seems to like me an awful lot. He ain't even tried to kiss me even tho I tried to let him know how bad I wanted him to. Just between us, diary. I think it ain't gonna be long fore he does it. I dream of him a kissin me. Maybe soon. He don't mentin a girlfriend or nuthin. So I guess ther ain't none. Talkin about him goin home makes me sad so we don't. I cain't wait fer tonite.

August 21st. Well diary, I got what I was hopin fer. Me and him got together last nite. I ain't ever been with no man before. Got started kissin and couldn't quit.

He had a lot to drink. I guess that gave him courage to do it. We sneaked in the back room while mama was drinkin with her friend, and I let him kiss me a long time. It felt so good to be loved. I ain't never been loved like he did me. I ain't never been told things like he told me. I know he loves me.

August 25th. Sorry I ain't wrote. I just don't know what happen to Randy. After that nite when we necked. He ain't acted rite. He speaks but won't be with me alone. Maybe he is aferd of mama. She can get mean. He jest acts so funny. Maybe I didn't do it rite and he don't like me no more. I have to aks im.

Sept. 1st. Randy's a comin back in to town tonite. Cain't wait to see him. I love him so much. Its hard a kepin this secret. I want to tell mama but she would shurly kill me and him.

Maybe one day I will be his wife. I dream of that all the time. At nite when I'm a layin in bed I think on the time he made me his. His lips were sa sweet an soft.

I looked at the clock and it was two thirty. I couldn't put the diary down, but somehow it seemed as if I was looking in on something I shouldn't see. I felt nauseated at the thought of my daddy with her, and too, knowing this was the time I was conceived. It's a shame he led her to believe he was single. He didn't lie, he just didn't tell the truth. *Withholding the truth still makes it a lie,* I reasoned to myself. There was love on one side as I was conceived. My mother seemed to have a good heart, just misplaced love. I got up and used the bathroom and took my seat again in the recliner. I just had to continue to read the story of my beginning.

The Moon Pie wrapper lay beside the empty Pepsi bottle. I would love to have another one, but I guess I would try to refrain. But my craving was coming back strong; I may just have to go to the pantry again. Oh well, maybe if I get back to reading I won't think about the Moon Pie.

Sept. 2nd. I guess I should start by sayin I'm powerful shamed of what happen with me n Randy last nite. I ain't tho because he loves me. I know fer sure now. We got to drinkin purty much. I don't usually drink but it sure did feel good. He tol me how much he missed me when he was gone and he couldn't do without me. We danced to the musik. The more we danced the closer he held me. The more we drank the better it felt. We was a lafin and havin so much fun. He pull me in the back room wher we done the kissin before. And one thing led to anuther and we didn't stop. It was diferent than I thought it would be. It hurt bad. But it felt good him bein my first tru love. Its rite it be hem. It was so wonderful bein loved. Now he would marry me fer sure. He didn't say, but thats what ya do when ya go all the way. He didn't say he loved me but I did hem. I know he does tho. I cain't wait fer tonite.

Sept. 30th. Its been a few day diary. Randy didn't come back and I'm so sad. I asked some of his budies and they said he just wanted to stay at camp by hisself. I got to go find out what happened. I miss him so bad.

I read on and on about her heartbreak because Daddy quit coming around. I guess his conscience got the best of him. I can see how unsaved people can fall to the demon of despair; I guess saved people do too. This was a classic story of a one night stand. She was looking for someone to love her and Daddy was looking for comfort in his grief. *If only he would have turned to Mama. Of course, I wouldn't be here,* I thought. Maybe Mama didn't know how to comfort him. I guess with Rose, she didn't ask questions.

It was now three o'clock, and I couldn't resist the call of the Moon Pie any longer. I tiptoed down the stairs to the kitchen one more time. I felt like a little kid with her hand in the cookie jar. I did decide to be a little good this time and got a tall glass of milk instead of Pepsi, and headed back to my reading. I was getting tired but couldn't put the diary down. Once settled, I picked up the yellowing pages and once again lost myself in her story.

Oct. 15th. I'm in big trubel, diary. I ain't come around this month. I'm almost two weeks late. That just ain't like me. I keep hopin' I will. I still ain't seen Randy. What will I do if I'm gona have his baby. Mama will kill me. I don't know how to go about gittin rid of it, plus I'm really skerd. Please come back Randy. I need you to hold me and tell me ever things gona be okay.

Nov. 15th. Well, diary there ain't no mistake I'm gonna have a baby. What am I gonna do. He wuz by the other nite and I was so happy til he tol me to ferget what ever hapen to us. That it wuz a big mistake, he wuz jist drunk and all. He said he wuz real sorry and didn't mean to hurt me none. My inside wuz like jelly. I wanted to cry real bad. I jist wish I coulda died. I'm awful sick, mama thinks I caut somethin. It won't be long for I have to tell her but I don't think I can.

Nov. 30th. I ben in bed sick fer 4 days. Mama guessed what was wrong when I werent trowin up or had a fever. She made me tell her who it was. I ain't never seen her so mad. She said she woud beat me if I wuznt so sick. We went to his bordin room and mama called him out. I didn't want to go but she made me get dresed and go. We stood ther in front of everbody and she told him. I thought I woud die frum shame. She jist told him he was a gonna be a daddy and aksed him whut was he gonna do bout it.

Whut happened next, diary, just kilt me. Mama told him he woud have to marry me. He said he cudnt cuz he were all ready marryed. He said he woud pay fer it but he cudnt leave his wife fer me. Mama wanted to kill him. If she had brung a gun she *said that woud be the last I seen of hem. I knew then I woud have a big job ahead of me.*

Jan. 28th. I'm already showin and I'm jist 4 month. Yer daddy is gone little one. Maybe some one will come along to love us one day and love us the rite way. I think I felt you move today. I Guess I'm alrite. Mama said I don't need no doctor since I'm feelin okay. She got a Granny comin when you get ready to come. Ya shore have been a movin taday. I'm feerd of what its gona be like. Mama said I wuz gona be in fer allful pain. She said aint no pain as bad. Thats my punishment. She said I was gona pay fer hurtin her the way I did. She cain't hole her head up no more. She won't let me go out wher anyone can see me. I stay back here in the back all the time. I git so lonely sometimes I jist sit and cry. Help me, diary.

My heart broke as I read what was happening to her. She tried to take care of me and love me. I can't imagine the loneliness she must have gone through. As I read of her baby kicking, I could feel my own moving. She was having twins and didn't even know. If she had, she would have been even more frightened. I continued on.

God Calls Our Name

May 20th I ain't got much longer. Your gittin to be such a big baby. I don't see how you can get much more bigger. They ain't much more room. I'm so sad and lonely I just want to die. Mama said I can go out after the youngun is born. She said she aint' gonna be imbarased by me. Its been a long time sinse I left these back rooms. I go out after dark and walk in the wouds. No body can see me then. I hate hidin. All I ever wanted was somebody to love me. I found a little Bible in one of the drawers. This Jesus sounds like someone that coud love me. I been reedin a lot lately cuz they ain't nuthin more to do. It says he loves bad people and can make all the bad good agin. It says if I talk to him he coud come in and live with me. I don't quite know how to do it but it sounds real good.

May 25th. Diary I ain't been doin' too good. I don't know if this Is the way yer posed to feel at the end. I so big I'm about to pop open. My feet and legs swoled up real bad. My hands is too time bigger. I don't look like me any more. No one coud love me the way I look cept my baby. I get skerder and skerder. I just don't see how that baby is gona come outa there. Baby I'm gona love you no matter whut. I won't be mean to ya. I'll make sure ya get a cake and maybe ice crem. You won't have a daddy but

God Calls Our Name

I'll be so good to you you won't ever be sad. I won't let no body hurt ya. I read in the bible today how Jesus loves little children. I know he loves me cuz his word say so. I need him so bad rite now cuz I ain't got no body. I akst him to come in my heart and you know whut? I know he did. This be the first time I ever felt loved. I gota tell mama about how Jesus loves her. Maybe it woud make her smile. I ain't ever seed her smile. I know he made me smile. God say he woud send his angels to be with me. I need em right now.

June 1st Mama says it may be any day you come little girl. I call you little girl. I hope yer a little girl. I sure feel bad. I jist don't see how I can go one more day. Mama says ats the way ever body feels when they like me. She says it will make me be a good girl from now on. I wern't bad afor, jist in love. I feel so sad. I wish I coud talk to some one. Mama don't let no body see me. I cry a lot, diary. I ain't seen no body sinse I started poochin' out to wher people knowed I wuz gona have a youngun. I'm locked up like an animal. I sure be glad when you get here baby. I don't know whut shes gona tell people when we have a baby runin round. I guess we will cross that bridge when we git thar if we ever git thar.

God Calls Our Name

June 2ˢᵗ. I woke up in awful pain this mornin. Mama sent fer granny Lucy. I hope she gets here fore you do little one. Diary, I been pledin with God to help me with the pain. I ain't had nuthin hurt this bad. I have to go now. I'll rite more later. I'm back, diary, still in bad pain. Mama says it always takes longer with the first one. I jist don't feel things is rite. I keep aksin mama fer a doc but she want get one. She says I'm just payen my dues fer sinin. Maybe she's rite. I keep aksin' God fer help but I don't think he heres me. If you love me God help me.

I wept as I read of the loneliness and pain she was going through. I'm glad I didn't read this before I got to know my grandmother or perhaps I wouldn't have been able to love her. How cruel she was to my mother. I wiped my eyes and began to read again.

June 23ʳᵈ. I aint' able to rite much. But I jist had to tell some body. I don't think they know whut they doin. They won't git me a doc. They jist tell me to shut up and stop hollern. The pain is so bad I think I mite die.

June 24ᵗʰ. I know sumpthin is awful rong. I'm bleeden real bad. I'm so week I caint hardly rite. I thout

64

that riten woud take my mind off it. I've beged God to take my life and not let me suffer any more. Me and my little one ain't gona make it. Lucy left and mama went to git…..

That was the last entry in her journal. What she must have suffered in the final days of her life. I know how very much she must have loved me. I'm glad my grandmother gave the diary to me. It must have been hard for her to know that I would read the full account. My heart just breaks for what she went through so that I could have life. I have to look at the fact that they are both saved and are in heaven. My grandmother is finally happy.

The next thing I remember is Daniel waking me up.

"Honey, have you been up all night?" he asked with concern.

"What time is it?"

"It's 7:00."

"Are you just getting home?" I asked.

"Yeah, it was a doozie of a night. I ended up having to do surgery too. I'm glad they called, it would have been impossible for them to do it all by themselves. I thought I kissed you goodbye in the bed. What happened?"

I held the notebook up for him to see. "I read my mother's diary. I just couldn't put it down once I started it. I wept through parts of it. It's kind of ironic that I was reading her account of my birth when I'm carrying twins of my own."

"You need to get to bed and sleep a little. Do you want something to eat first?" he asked, pulling me to my feet.

He glanced at the table beside the chair. "Two Moon Pies, you had two Moon Pies?" he asked as I buried my head in his chest.

"I was craving them so bad. But I did have milk with one instead of Pepsi," I said, proud of myself.

"I'm going to have to take an extra job to keep you in Moon Pies. I bet we have some sweet children the way you love sugar."

"I'm going to weigh two hundred pounds by the time they come. Why couldn't I have craved celery?"

"Come, my little Moon Pie, let's me and you go to bed."

"Are we getting a little romantic?" I asked, smiling at him.

"No, we're getting a lot sleepy," he said, diving under the covers. "Come lay down with me. I rest so much better when you're beside me."

I cuddled up near him and was glad to be going back to sleep. As soon and I got comfortable and was drifting off, the little football players started their line up and began kicking at the same time. "The joys of motherhood," I muttered, turning over to reposition them.

Chapter Five

It was late November and I was getting huge. The babies moved constantly. I don't think they ever slept at the same time. I couldn't find any way to get comfortable, and I still had a month to go. Dr. Roger, as I fondly called him, said I was doing great. My weight gain was right on target despite the Moon Pie craving. Roger wasn't too pleased with what I was craving. He teased me every time I went in to be checked. We were planning a C-section the third week in December. I hated that it would be so close to Christmas, but that is the way God planned it. He warned me I might go into labor spontaneously and would need to get to the hospital immediately. Chris was due to be present at the delivery. He was still concerned about the possible weakness in the artery in the back of my head, so he kept close vigil on me, too. He had a whole case of Moon Pies and a carton of Pepsi waiting for me my last visit. He made me swear not to tell anyone he got them for me. I was their office joke, I'm sure, but it was all done in love. I had already gained sixty pounds but was promised it was mostly babies. We would definitely find out soon. Daniel and one of the new doctors were scheduled to go on one of the mountain trips. I hated for him to go so late in my pregnancy, but he swore he could get back in time to be present for the birth.

I was getting ready for Christmas, and Mandy was helping me get the house decorated. She was so talented I pretty much just turned her loose. We started right after Thanksgiving putting things up around the house. The tree would be up soon. I remembered going with Daniel last year to cut trees, but that was not to be this year.

Daniel got up early to go into a new community they had been referred to. Both doctors were so excited about it I hated to ask him not to go. They promised to be back by nightfall. The community that we first visited was doing well. Essie had gotten extensive counseling for the abuse she encountered, and was doing well and Iona never regretted calling us for help. Essie returned home after about six weeks of intense therapy and because she stuck with the whole program, the kids were given back to her. The children healed exceptionally well for all they had been through, and seemed to be happy. Maybe the cycle of abuse was going to finally be stopped. We had a lot of people coming in for treatment, which is good. They no longer fear the new doctors.

I was sitting on my balcony enjoying the afternoon sun, when Mandy came to me with a phone call. It was Darrel calling about Daddy John. He said he wasn't doing well and was asking if I could come and check on him. I knew Daniel didn't want me driving but Darrel sounded so desperate, and the distance was short between our houses.

"I'll be right there," I heard myself tell him.

Mandy was standing within earshot and had heard what I said.

"You're not going off by yerself, Missy. Daniel would have our hides. Where you go, I go. He told me not to leave yer side," she said adamantly.

"Okay, but we have to go right away."

We made it to the house in a matter of minutes. Darrel was waiting for us on the porch.

"Hurry, 'Lisbeth, Daddy's not doin' good a tall," he said with a worried look on his face.

We made our way into the back room where Daniel had delivered Sharon's babies. I went over to the bed and eased my large frame down by his side. I took my stethoscope and blood pressure cuff with me. He was barely conscious.

"Daddy John, can you hear me? This is Elizabeth. I came to see how you're doing. Can you hear me?"

He turned his head in my direction and barely opened his eyes.

"I'm so glad ya come, chile. I do feel poorly. I feel I ain't long fer dis place. Joy comin', joy comin', mornin' jest bout here, 'Lis'beth Ann."

The beating of his heart was so slow, and very shallow, and I knew he was right about not being here long.

"Daddy John, we need to call an ambulance. You're real sick."

He raised his hand weakly and waved me off, "No time fer it. I'm goin' home, 'Lisbeth Ann, I'm going home. It's mornin' time and I'm goin' home." he said, barely above a whisper.

I went out on the porch and talked to the boys, and suggested they go say goodbye. They walked dejectedly down the hall to their father's bedside. I could hear their sobbing and I couldn't hold back my own tears at that point. My resolve to hold it all together came crashing down. I could hear their voices break as they talked to him through their sobs. He had gone through so much heartache and physical pain, but always managed to keep a smile on his sweet face.

Mandy stood with her arm around my shoulder and tried to keep me calm.

"You okay, Missy?" she asked me several times. "Master Daniel gonna kill me dis time. I know he gonna be mad."

"I'm fine, I'm going to try to call Daniel and see if he's back from his run up in the mountains."

I called the office and his secretary told me he was there but not inside. She would have to go get him to call me right back.

He must have been where he could answer the phone in the RV, because he called back almost immediately.

"Are you okay, honey?"

"Daniel," was all I managed to get out because of my sobs. I couldn't even tell him what happened, and Mandy took the phone from me.

"Master Daniel, Daddy John jist up 'n died and me and 'Lis'beth had to come help him. And she got real upset when he died on her. Ya need to get on over here."

She turned to tell me what he said.

"He said he would call the coroner and git them to come to the house and dat he would be right here. He ain't none happy wit me," she said, shaking her head. "Oh, Master Daniel gonna kill me dis time."

I sat on the porch in the swing waiting for him to come. It had been unusually warm for December, but they were calling for a drastic change for tomorrow. The cool air felt good on my face. Maybe if the weather turned cold the swelling would go down in my feet.

From the time he called, it took about fifteen minutes for him to get there. I could see the dust rising from his car as he came up the little dirt road. He was out of the car in an instant and came bounding up the steps to where I was sitting. He gave Mandy an exasperated look and turned to me.

He came and knelt down in front of me.

"I'm furious with you. Do you know that?"

I had never seen Daniel so upset with me.

"Daddy John was calling for me. Darrel was so desperate I had to come to him," I said with a fresh flow of tears starting. "I'm fine. I was just upset that he died. I thought I could talk him into coming to see you."

"Why didn't you call me to come check him?"

"Because, I knew you were still on your trip. I just reacted to the emergency. I'm sorry, I wasn't thinking. Would you go check on the twins? They've been in there for a long time."

"Don't change the subject; you could have made yourself go into labor. You scare me sometimes, Libby," he said, pulling me as best he could into his arms. "And yes, I will go check on the boys," he said emphatically.

He went to the bed where Daddy John was lying. Darrel was sitting in a chair near the bed crying softly now. David was on the other side of the bed just staring at his father. Daniel checked for a pulse, and confirmed what we already knew, that he indeed had passed away. He led the boys out to the living room, and talked to them for a while. They seemed to be doing much better by the time he finished. He turned and came to where I was sitting.

"Are you sure you're feeling okay?" he asked worriedly.

"Yeah, I'm sure. I'm sorry, Daniel. I really didn't mean to worry you."

"Promise me you won't do anything foolish again. You're driving me nuts." It was obvious he still wasn't completely over his scare.

"I promise I'll be a good girl. Now would you help me up?" I said, smiling at him.

Daniel pulled me to my feet and the three of us made our way outside to our vehicles.

"Mandy, you ride with me and Libby; I'll get Chris to come drive the car home."

"Daniel, I can drive. I really do feel okay."

"Master Daniel, don't go gettin' all mad at us. We jist had to come to Daddy John."

"I'm not mad. I just worry about Libby and the babies," he said, still not very happy with the two of us.

He relented and I drove Mandy and me home, while Daniel followed close behind. When we got to our house he asked me to come up to our bedroom. He wanted to talk to me. He sat me down on the bed and took my shoes off. He had me put my feet up and lay down on the bed beside me.

"You scared me so bad when I called, and you were crying so hard I didn't know what had happened. I thought you and the babies were in trouble," he said, brushing my hair back from my face.

"I'm so sorry, sweetheart. I really didn't mean to upset you."

"It's not about upsetting me; it's about putting yourself in danger."

"I didn't think about it being dangerous. I just needed to get to Daddy John. He was like a father to me."

"If anything happened to you or the babies, I don't know what I would do," he said, with tears welling in his eyes.

"We're going to be okay, honey. God is taking care of us."

"I've got to get back to the clinic. You stay put, young lady. I'll try to be home early."

He leaned down and gave me and the babies a kiss.

"I love you, try to get some rest."

I lay there and thought about Daddy John in the portals of heaven. I could see the sweet reunion between him, Bessie and his grandbaby. It was awfully hard to be sad when he was finally home. I was sad for the boys, but God would take care of them. They had each other and Sharon had Ralph and the baby. He was such a kind soul and would be missed by everyone here in these mountains. In the eighty years God had given him, he never once left the mountains.

Chapter Six

As I was lying there I felt a sudden heaviness in the lower part of my stomach. Several times my whole abdomen tightened and hardened. Probably all the standing I had done today. I knew my feet were swollen, so maybe this was just a reaction to all the stress.

I'm not sure at what point I went to sleep, but I didn't wake up until Daniel woke me for dinner.

"How is my princess?" he asked as he kissed me.

"Am I still your princess?"

"Always," he said, kissing me long and tenderly.

"I'm just very tired. The babies move and kick constantly. It's really hard for me to get in any position to rest. I probably won't feel any better until they come."

I felt my stomach tighten and become real hard again. It was much harder this time, even though there was still no pain. I closed my eyes and lay my head back on the pillow.

"Give me your hand, honey; I want you to feel something. I don't want to alarm you, but I think I'm having a contraction."

"Tell me what it feels like," he said excitedly.

"It's passed now, but my stomach gets real hard for a few seconds and then it relaxes."

"When did this start?"

"Earlier, when I was trying to go to sleep, I felt the first one. Please don't tell me I told you so," I said pleadingly.

"The next one you have, tell me." He checked his watch and mentally recorded the time.

He crawled up in bed beside me, and we waited anxiously to see if it was going to happen again.

"I'm going to go ask Mandy to bring our dinner up here."

He had just gotten back to the bed when it happened again.

"Daniel, it's happening," I said, putting my hands over my stomach.

He sat down on the side of the bed and pulled up my top. He felt all around as I had the contraction.

"Oh man, it's hard as a rock. Let me time it."

He looked at his watch and felt my stomach as the contraction continued.

"Two minutes."

"Do you think it's labor, honey?" I asked expectantly.

"I hope not. It's too early," he said. "As long as they aren't accompanied by pain I think you're okay."

There was a light knock on the door and Mandy came in with our dinner tray. Daniel helped her set it up on a small table in our room. I tried to get up to eat but couldn't. I wasn't hungry at all.

"I don't think I want to eat right now."

He brought me a half of a sandwich and made me eat it.

"You've got to eat, honey. You can't let yourself get down. How about a Moon Pie?" he asked, grinning at me.

"No," I said, laughing at him. "Not even a Moon Pie."

Daniel ate while keeping a close watch on me.

"Turn over on your side when you have your next contraction. If it's false labor, it will stop. Maybe a nice warm bath would help. Oh, that's right. You can't get out of the tub, silly me."

"Daniel, come lie down with me when you finish eating."

"I'm going to go take a shower first. I need to get some of the day's grime off me."

He headed for the shower while I tried to rest. I had one more contraction while he was in the shower.

He turned the overhead light off and turned the bedside lights on. He got his Bible off his dresser and read to me for a while. The more he read, the sleepier I got. He read to me out of the Psalms. They were always soothing to me. I didn't awake until the middle of the night when I had to go to the bathroom.

Daniel snapped awake when the mattress shifted as I got out of bed.

"Where are you going, honey? Are you okay?" he asked sleepily.

"I'm fine, just going to the bathroom."

"Any more contractions?" he inquired.

"No, I haven't had any for a while."

"Good, that's real good news."

Daniel was up early the next morning and had to leave before long to do hospital rounds. I was awake when he got ready to leave.

"I want you to stay in bed today and call me if there is any change. I'll tell Dan what's been happening. He might want you to come in for a check up. If he does, I'll swing by and pick you up. Karen can page me if I need to be reached."

It was a dark cold rainy day. It had rained all night, and was supposed to turn to snow later. They were calling for snow in and around our area.

I said a silent prayer for Daniel that God would keep him safe as he traveled the back roads today.

I tried to go back to sleep, but to no avail. I twisted and turned, and plumped and fluffed my pillows. I stuffed them under my legs, and arms, but was still restless. Mandy came in and checked on me. She came up with a full breakfast tray.

"Master Daniel said I was to make sure you eat sumpthin' this mornin'," she said, arranging my food for me. "I'm gonna start you a nice warm fire in the fireplace. I know how much you like dat. It might make you feel better."

"I'll try eating something, Mandy, but I'm so miserable I don't know if I can eat much."

"Well, jist try."

"Mandy, would you call Daddy John's house and tell Sharon I won't be able to come to the funeral home. Tell her Daddy Daniel ordered me to bed today."

"I'll go do that right now."

The contractions were nagging and beginning to feel uncomfortable now and had moved to the lower part of my stomach like I was going to start my period. I felt I should call Roger and tell him what was going on. I'm sure Daniel had already given him an ear full.

I called his office, and his nurse said he was at the hospital with a complicated delivery and they weren't sure when he would be back. I explained I was having some discomfort in the bottom part of my stomach and the hardness that I was having. She proceeded to explain the fact that false labor wasn't unusual and that's probably all it was. If I had any spotting, or a sudden gush of water, or if the tightening became more uncomfortable, I was to come in as soon as possible.

Oh, well, I thought, *I'll just do as Daniel said and lie here and rest.* I turned on the TV to the local news. They had just done a weather bulletin and it sounded like we were in for some bad weather. Snow was definitely called for in our area. I had just gotten settled and was going to watch a movie that was coming on when I heard it start to thunder. *That's weird,* I thought, *you don't often hear thunder during a snowstorm.* There were several big claps right in a row. I got up to go look out the French doors and the lights went out.

Oh great, that's just what I need, a day without electricity. I headed to the bathroom again. Just as I reached for the door, a gush of water came from me. I yelled for Mandy as I made my way to the commode.

"I know. I'm comin' with the lantern," she said as she came into the bedroom.

"I'm in here, and I think my water has broken," I said with a panicked voice.

"Ya sure?" she questioned.

"Oh yeah, I'm pretty positive. It's all over the floor. Be careful where you're stepping. We've got to call Daniel..., no we've got to call Roger..., try Dr. Roger at the office and tell them to call Daniel. They have a beeper number for him."

"I called Dr. Dan and they says he still at the hospital, fer you to go right there."

"And how am I supposed to get there? I can't drive," I said, exasperated.

"Oh, Missy! What we gonna do?"

"Try to call Daniel's mom and dad," I told her.

Mandy returned into the room with the news.

"Mrs. Scott's at the doctor with Grandma and Mr. Scott he gone over to the next county fer supplies. The boy what answered the phone say he will tell her as soon as she gets back."

"Did you say it was an emergency?"

"I said the babies is a comin'." Her voice was quivering.

"I've got to stay calm," I said, taking a deep breath. "I've got to think, I've got to think," I kept telling myself.

The phone ringing beside my bed made me jump. I grabbed it on the first ring.

"Hello."

"Hey, honey, I just got the beep. What's wrong?"

"My water just broke, and I don't know what to do," I said, starting to cry. "It has started to snow pretty hard and we don't have any power."

"Honey, are you sure your water broke?"

"Oh yeah, it went everywhere," I said, trying to get calmed down.

"Listen, I want you to go lie down on the bed. Tell Mandy to start a fire in the fireplace to keep the room warm.

"We have to detour because a bridge is out. I'll call Chris and have him come. He can probably make it quicker than I can. I'll send him with an ambulance. Stay calm. How close are the contractions?"

"About ten minutes, I think. They're starting to get more painful and I feel a lot of pressure. Oh....Daniel here comes another one," I said, gripping the side of the bed with my free hand.

"Chris should be there with you in just a few minutes. Don't panic, okay? As soon as I can get there, I will. I love you, honey."

"I love you too, but I'm really scared. What if he doesn't make it?" I implored.

"Let me go, I've got to go call Chris. I'll call you back."

"Bye." I heard the phone click and the dial tone came on the line.

I hung up the phone and lay back on the propped-up pillows. I wanted desperately to cry, but forced myself to stay calm. As another contraction hit, my resolve was diminishing. It was much more painful this time. I knew they meant business about coming out. I grabbed for Mandy's hand.

"Missy, what did Master Daniel say?" she said, her eyes as large as saucers.

"Have you ever delivered a baby, Mandy?" I asked her calmly.

"No. Missy, and I ain't ever seen one born either. I don't think that's what you want to hear." She was stiff with fright.

"I think you better pray that Chris gets here before these babies do."

Mandy's prayer was short and to the point, asking God to send someone quickly, and to hold the babies back.

"Oh, Mandy, here comes another one! It couldn't have been ten minutes yet."

She went and got a washcloth to wipe my face. I felt hot and clammy. She held my hand as I cried out in pain.

"They seem to be lasting longer than before," I said breathlessly to Mandy.

The phone rang again. I picked it up before it could finish the first ring.

"Daniel!" I yelled into the phone. "You've got to hurry, honey. It's getting bad."

"This isn't Daniel, it's Chris, I'm on my way. Listen to me carefully. I should be there in about ten to fifteen minutes. I'm driving and the ambulance is coming behind me. When did you have your last contraction?"

"One just finished. They're hard, Chris. You need to hurry. The pain is really bad now. I don't know what to do!" I cried into the phone.

"Give the phone to Mandy. I need to tell her what to do, just in case."

"Just in case what?" I yelled.

"I'll get there, don't…"

The phone went dead about the time a loud clap of thunder sounded. A rare thunder snow shower!

"It's dead! We don't even have a phone. Here comes another one, Mandy."

"Jus' hold my hand, honey, and squeeze all you want to; you ain't gonna hurt me."

"Pray again, Mandy, pray again." I pleaded.

"I ain't quit a prayin', chile, I ain't quit."

When the pain subsided I took some long slow breaths, willing myself not to panic anymore than I already had.

"Go into the nursery and get a couple baby blankets out of the drawer. In the hall closet are some old sheets you can put under me." She went without hesitation.

When she came back she placed the sheets and plastic bag under me and helped me change into a clean gown. The one I had on was wet from where my water broke.

It had been an hour since I talked with Daniel, and it had been twenty minutes since I talked with Chris. "What is keeping him?" I thought out loud. Another pain gripped my midsection. I grabbed the headboard of the bed and pulled to help ease the pain.

"He's here, Missy, Chris is here. Thank you, Jesus," she said, running into the bedroom.

No sooner had she uttered those words than he dashed in behind her.

"Boy, you sure know how to shake things up, sweetie."

"Mandy, bring that light over here and hold it where I can see what I'm doing," he said, snapping his gloves over his hands.

He was examining me when another contraction hit.

"Help me! It's coming again!" I screamed at him.

"Well would you look at this, he's crowned! One big push and we're going to have a baby."

Right now, it's coming now?" I asked. "What about the hospital?"

"Afraid not. It's just you and me, kiddo."

"Here it comes. I've got to push."

"Go ahead, push it out. Push hard, push..." he encouraged.

"Pull it out!" I screamed at him. "Just pull it out."

"One more big push like that one and we'll have a baby," he said.

"You said that last time," I screamed at him.

"Listen to me, sweetie. I can't pull it out; you're going to push it out. You have to trust me. I have to work the shoulders a little and it will be here. I think we have a football player. I've done this before, and you're doing great."

I screamed as another pain gripped me. "I'm not great, I'm not great."

"If you put the energy into pushing and not screaming. Push... push harder."

"I can't push any harder," I yelled at him when the pain ended. "I bet if you were on this end you would scream."

"I think with the next one it will be here."

"Okay, I'll try, but what will happen if I can't push it out."

"That's not an option; you're going to push it out," he declared.

"Mandy, put the lantern down and help her move down to where she can put her feet on the foot board so she can push against it. That will help the baby move."

Mandy got the sheet and pulled me down to where I could put my feet up.

"Oh, God, please help me," I said, as the pain overtook me. I pushed with my feet as hard as I could.

"Here it comes." Chris said, as the baby slid out into his hands.

"What is it?" I asked.

"You've got a baby girl."

"I didn't hear her cry. Is she okay?"

"Yeah, she's okay. She's breathing, just not crying yet. I'm going to do a little suctioning."

I heard a squeaky little cry come from her, and it was music to my ears.

"She's singing now," Chris said.

"I've never heard a prettier song."

"Let Uncle Chris cut the cord and we'll get ready for your brother or sister." he said, talking to the baby.

"Mandy, do you have something to put around the baby?"

"Here's a baby blanket."

"Come here and take the baby," he said, placing her into Mandy's arms.

"It may take just a little bit for the next baby to move down into position. It won't be long though, maybe about two or three minutes."

I felt another strong contraction coming.

"Here it comes, Chris. I can't take any more," I moaned.

"Sure you can, we're almost there now. Big sister's already made a runway. It's coming down nicely. One more contraction like that one and it should slip right out.

"Don't lie to me, Chris."

"I wouldn't lie to you, honey."

I heard a commotion at the door; suddenly, Daniel was at my side.

"Hey, Daddy, you got here just in time to help me."

"What do you want me to do?" Daniel asked.

"I want you to look right here."

"Oh, my! It's the head."

"Yep, it's a head. I want you to put your gloves on right quick and deliver your baby."

"Me, you want *me* to?"

"Do you think you can handle it, Dr. Scott?" Chris said, smiling at Daniel. "You have delivered babies before, haven't you?"

"Not my own. Believe me, it's a whole different perspective."

"One of you better do it, because it's coming."

I heard Daniel as he pulled the gloves into place over his hands. Chris moved over so Daniel could move in. I screamed out as the baby moved down the birth canal.

"Push," Chris commanded, "push like you mean it!"

I pushed with all the strength I had and still no second baby.

"I can't do this again. I can't do it again, I'm just too tired," I said weakly.

"With the next contraction you will have it, so push real hard. Push with your feet like you did before."

"The head is right here, honey," Daniel said.

"We had a little trouble with the wide shoulders with the other baby. I think this one may come on down," Chris said.

The lights came on and the brightness filled the room. A contraction hit, and with all the strength I had, I pushed. The baby slipped out into Daniel's hands.

"We have a boy, honey, we have a boy," he said, as he suctioned his mouth and nose. The baby gave a loud resounding cry.

"He has good lungs," Chris said. "His little sister wasn't so vocal."

Chris handed Daniel the forceps to cut the cord.

"Honey, you're doing great. You're almost through, the rest won't be bad."

"I'm so tired. Please tell me it's over."

Chris took my little girl and laid her in my arms. "Here you go, Mama. This will make you feel better."

"She is so beautiful. Look at her dark hair. Look, honey, she looks just like you."

"Move over and I will finish here for you," Chris said to Daniel.

Mandy handed the little boy to Daniel. He was screaming at the top of his lungs.

"Don't cry, little fella. This is Daddy, its okay. Do you want to see your beautiful mama?" Daniel lowered the baby so I could see him.

"Daniel, he looks just like his sister. A girl and a boy, and they're both perfect," I said, still in awe of what had come out of my body.

"The ambulance attendants are downstairs," Mandy said, entering the room.

"I'll go tell them we'll have her ready for transfer in a jiffy," Chris said, heading for the stairs.

"How are you doing, honey?" Daniel asked, coming to my side. "I'm so proud of you. You did a terrific job," he said, as he kissed me gently on the lips. Our little girl let out a scream as he did.

"She's already a jealous little female," he said, giving her a kiss.

"I'm feeling fine right now. How do you think I'm doing, doctor?" I asked Chris as he walked back into the room.

"You're doing great. Things couldn't have gone better, except if it had all taken place in a delivery room. You were a real trooper."

"I'm sorry I screamed at you," I said, laughing at him.

"I was too busy to notice," he said, winking at me.

"You've come to my rescue twice. I owe you once again."

"You don't owe me anything. God just put Uncle Chris in the right place at the right time. I think you did this to escape a C-section," he said, laughing at me.

Daniel cuddled our little boy close to him, rocking him back and forth in his arms.

"I was terrified when you called," he said, looking at me. "I couldn't do anything but pray. I didn't think I was ever going to get here. The roads were getting icy and we couldn't go any faster than we were. I never want to go through anything like that again."

"You?" I said.

"Yeah, I was doing fine in life until you came along, and turned everything upside down. You've made me a beautiful wife and given me two beautiful children. But, boy, have you made me work for it."

"And not to mention what she's put Uncle Chris through. Wait until I tell the babies how they got here."

"I'm just glad you made it. I don't think Mandy was in any shape to do a delivery."

"I woulda done it, to hep you get 'em here, I jist thank God fer Dr. Chris. I ain't ever seed nothin more beautiful than him comin' up dem steps," Mandy piped up from the doorway.

"We need to get her and the babies to the hospital. It's gotten real cold out, so make sure we get them all bundled up good."

"Are you ready to go, princess?" Daniel said. "And are you ready to go, my little prince and princess?" he said, with a baby in each arm.

"I don't want to go to the hospital, do you think it's necessary.

Chris brought the stretcher.

"I think I could stand up and get on it. I'm not helpless."

"Okay, honey, if that would be better for you, you can," he said, offering me his arm.

"Steady yourself just a bit before you walk. You might be light-headed."

Chris helped me onto the stretcher and covered me with a warm blanket. Daniel placed a baby in each arm and pushed the stretcher to the stairs.

"I think I'll carry the babies down instead of putting them on the stretcher," Chris said, taking the babies from me.

He handed Mandy the little boy and he took the little girl. As we entered the kitchen, Daniel's mom and dad greeted us.

"We got here as fast as we could. Are ya alright?" his mom asked, coming to the stretcher.

"I am now. Chris got here in time to deliver the babies."

Daniel took the babies one by one and laid them in his parents' arms. He was grinning from ear to ear.

"This one is a boy and this one is a girl."

"What are their names?" his dad inquired.

"We haven't named them yet."

His mom and dad just beamed over them. Each parent had one in their arms cooing over them.

"Well, I hate to have to speed up your visit but we've got to get them to the hospital to be cleaned up and weighed. And we need to get Libby checked out," Chris said, ushering us toward the door.

After a round of kisses we were out the door to the waiting ambulance. Daniel rode in the back with me. He held one of the babies and I held one.

"We got November babies instead of December babies," I told Daniel once we were settled in for the ride to the hospital.

"They are *so* cute, honey. I can't get over how precious they are," he said, wiping tears from his eyes. "Just think; our love created them."

I reached over top of the stretcher to brush the tears from his cheek. "Yeah, with a little help from God."

"I still can't believe it's over," he said.

"I can't believe all this came out of me."

"I was terrified for you. I knew when you told me your water broke it could go fast. I was just praying God would be with you and Chris would get there before they came."

"Your worst nightmare came true."

"What's that?"

"Having a delivery at home."

Chris swung open the back doors as soon as we got to the ambulance entrance.

"I need to take Libby in and make sure everything is going good. Roger is supposed to meet us here. You can take the babies up to the nursery and get them checked in," he said to Daniel.

"Yes sir," Daniel said. "You just really take charge."

"Only when I have to."

The snow had been coming down pretty steady, and the flakes were still falling as they unloaded me. One big fat flake landed squarely on my nose. They hurried me into the warmth of the hospital. Daniel came and kissed me goodbye.

"I'll be back to you as soon as possible. I'll stay with the babies until they are through checking them, and then I'll bring them back to you."

"Promise?"

"I promise," he said kissing me again.

Daniel headed up to the nursery with the babies.

"I guess that just leaves me and you kid," Chris said, smiling at me.

"Yeah, just me and you kid," I said, smiling back at him.

He pushed me into one of the exam rooms and asked the nurse to clean me up.

She brought a basin of warm water to the bedside and gave me a bath from head to toe. It felt so good to be at peace again. The whole episode was terrifying, but God had brought me through it safely. Once the nurse had me bathed and in a clean gown, Chris came in and checked me over.

"You're doing excellent. I'm glad you didn't have to push very long. I was concerned about pressure on your head, but that didn't seem to present a problem."

"Were you nervous?" I asked him.

"I was shaking like a leaf, but you're not supposed to tell your patients that. If it had been someone I didn't know it would have been much easier. I was just hoping all I would have to do is catch them when they slid out, which is what I did. You did all the work. I wish you could have seen

Daniel's face when he saw the head of the baby right there ready to come out. It was priceless. I wish I had had a camera. I was hoping to be present for the delivery but not to do the delivering."

"What would I have done without you?" I said, stretching out my hand for him to hold.

"God would have sent an angel," he said, kissing my fingers.

"He did send an angel."

"Let's get you up to a room so you can be with Daddy and the babies."

He took me up, and got me settled into a comfortable bed.

"I'll be right back, sweetie, I've got to go give the nurses some orders and tell Roger where you are."

I closed my eyes and drifted off to sleep. When I woke up, Daniel and Chris were coming in with the babies in their isolettes.

"Uncle Chris has already got a good start taking care of you little guys," he said to the baby.

"How much did they weigh?" I asked Daniel.

"Our son weighed 5 pounds, 3 ounces and is 19 inches long. Our little princess weighed in at 5 pounds, 6 ounces and is 20 inches long. I told the nurse I had to get the stats down because that's the first thing you would ask."

"I think we need to give them names, don't you?"

"Do you have any suggestions?" Daniel asked.

"Well, as I was drifting off to sleep awhile ago I was thinking about their names. I thought about my two mothers' names and came up with Rose Mary. What do you think of that?"

As he cuddled his new daughter in his arms, he whispered over and over, "Rose Mary Scott. That's a beautiful name. You'll always be Daddy's little rose bud."

"And our son, I think I have a name for him you will like. I was thinking Daniel Christopher, after his daddy and Uncle Chris."

"They are like soft little kittens," Daniel commented.

The soft drone of their voices lulled me to sleep. When I woke up sometime during the night, the babies weren't in the room. Daniel was asleep in the chair by my bed.

"Daniel, I need to get up and go to the bathroom," I said to him.

He lowered the bed rails and helped me to the bathroom.

"How did everything go?" he said when I finished.

"Not as bad as I thought it would be," I said, making my way back to the bed.

"We didn't have to do an episiotomy, so you shouldn't be as sore as you could have been."

"I beg to differ," I said, smiling at him. "It isn't your bottom."

"Thank God," he said.

The nurse poked her head in the door.

"Mrs. Scott, are you up to a feeding? One little native is getting restless."

"Sure."

She handed her to me and helped me get her positioned to feed.

"Danny is still sleeping, so you can feed Rose Mary."

Daniel moved up beside me and watched as I fed her.

"You're so beautiful," he said.

When I finished feeding Rose Mary the nurse came in with Danny.

"He was wide awake and wanted to join the family," she said, placing him in my arms.

He got the hang of it pretty quick and latched on hungrily.

"You might have to supplement with a bottle. Maybe take turns feeding them. You don't want to become latched to them twenty-four hours a day, and I'm not sure you could produce enough milk for two," she said as she left the room.

"Thanks," I called after her.

Daniel took Rose Mary and laid her in the bassinet and then took Danny from my arms. He held him up where he could look into his little face.

"I hope I can be to you what God wants me to be. I pray you grow up to be a strong man one day, someone that loves God with all his heart." He pulled Danny close to him and kissed him. "How can one man be so blessed? He's so beautiful, honey," he said, looking first at his son and then at me.

"If he turns out like his father, he will be wonderful."

"Just think, this time last year we were just getting to know each other, and now we've produced two beautiful children."

"I still can't believe it sometimes." He called for the nurse to come take the babies back to the nursery. When they were safely in the nurse's care,

Daniel came and lay down beside me on my bed. He pulled me close to him and kissed me.

"Just close your eyes and rest. I will always take care of you and the babies."

Epilogue

It seems like a lifetime ago that I began my journey home. I ran from these beloved mountains for years hoping to excise all of the oppression that was in this place. I fought hard to escape and was happy when my dreams became a reality. I was searching for a place filled with wonder and excitement. But for some reason the wonder and excitement of what I found in the city didn't purge the past that haunted me.

I love to sit here in the gazebo swing and watch the seasons change. This has to be my favorite place in the whole world.

Each season has its own special beauty. Fall comes and dresses the mountains in a brilliant array of colors. A patchwork quilt of splendor spread out before me. The animals scurry about, storing their harvest for the winter food. The birds fly in huge flocks, too many to number. The geese come in their unmistakable "v" shape, honking as they go in search of warm weather. How could one not believe in God when you view these things? Who but God could tell them how to fly and where to fly?

The Indian summer comes and fog shrouds the valley below. The warmth of the earth colliding with the cool nights produces the fog. My daddy used to say if you count the number of foggy mornings in September you would know how many times it would snow in the winter.

As winter comes, the patchwork of the quilt becomes a blanket of white. The animals are tucked into their beds to wait for spring. Smoke spirals up from the chimneys of the cabins on the valley floor below. Each one representing people that Daniel and I came here to love and care for.

Then the signal comes and spring bursts forth. The forest comes alive again with buds on the trees and berries starting on the vine. The mountains break forth in a symphony of song. The birds sing and tree frogs croak. Each insect has its own specific melody to play in this wonderful concerto.

The cycle begins again just as God has commanded it.

The trees shed leaves, plants drop their seedlings; and from death, springs life, anew, when God signals the earth to warm and the cycle of life begins again.

The farmer readies his land for the seeds that the spring rain and summer sun will bring to fruition. I love the smell of honeysuckle wafting up the mountainside. It must be a sweet savor in the nostrils of God. The berry vines are full of blooms, with each one representing a big plump berry. This ridge is full of berry vines just as Daniel said when we hunted our first Christmas tree.

Blackberry Ridge is an appropriate name for our mountaintop home place. His grandfather would have loved what Daniel has done here. The apple trees are full of blooms, and will bear fruit well into the fall.

God Calls Our Name

Ah yes, summer...how I love to sit here among the cool trees and watch Danny and Rose Mary play. They are already two years old. Where has the time gone? It seems like it was just yesterday when they made their speedy arrival.

Daniel and Chris have made giant strides in the care of the mountain people. They have begun to get used to the young doctors and their specialties. The medical van still goes on its monthly trips. The doctors all look forward to their turn coming. The twins and I go with Daniel on some of his short trips. The people just love the babies and Daddy likes showing them off. He has me bring them to the office to visit him for lunch so everyone can see them.

No, God did not forsake these hills as I foolishly said in my youth. I was the one that forsook them. God opened my eyes to their beauty. How could I have been afraid to come back to them?

God's blessings have been abundant in my life here with Daniel and the twins. As great as my despair was when I lost David, God has matched with happiness with Daniel.

Joy does come in the morning Daddy John, joy does come in the morning.

www.ingramcontent.com/pod-product-compliance
Lightning Source LLC
Chambersburg PA
CBHW071405170626
46811CB00003B/1266